D1146574

# THIS BOOK BELONGS TO

Published by BBC Books,
a division of BBC Enterprises Limited,
Woodlands, 80 Wood Lane, London W12 OTT

First published 1949 by Sampson Lowe as *Little Noddy Goes to Toyland*.

First published by BBC Books in paperback 1992
Reprinted 1993
© Darrell Waters Limited 1949 as to all text and illustrations

Enid Blyton's signature mark and the word 'NODDY'
are Registered Trade Marks of Darrell Waters Limited

ISBN 0 563 36800 4

Printed and bound in Great Britain by BPCC Hazells Limited Member of BPCC

# NODDY GOES TO TOYLAND

BY Enid Blyton

## CONTENTS

Pictures by Beek

BBC BOOKS

THE MARKET WAS A LOVELY PLACE, AND VERY BUSY

## BIG-EARS GETS A SURPRISE

BIG-EARS the brownie was hurrying through the woods on his little red bicycle, when he suddenly bumped into somebody.

Down they went, and the bicycle fell on top of Big-Ears with a crash.

"Ooooh!" he said, and rubbed the bump on his head.

"Ooooh!" said the person he had bumped into, and sat up to look at Big-Ears. Big-Ears looked at him, too.

"You're rather a peculiar-looking person," said Big-Ears, staring. "What are you? You're not a pixie or a brownie or a goblin, are you?"

"No," said the person he had knocked over, nodding his head.

"Are you a toy?" asked Big-Ears. "I've never seen one quite like you."

"No, I don't think so," said the strange person, nodding his head.

"Why do you nod your head when you say 'No'?" asked Big-Ears, still staring.

"Because I'm a little nodding man," said the small fellow. "My head's balanced on my neck in such a way that I have to nod when I speak. Oooh—what's that? Is it somebody after me?"

"No. It's only a field-mouse scurrying by," said Big-Ears, getting up. "Where do you live? And why are you afraid of somebody coming after you?"

"Because I've run away!" said the nodding

8

man. "I belonged to Old Man Carver, away in the woods, you know. He made me."

"Did he really?" said Big-Ears. "How did he make you?"

"He made wooden feet, and then wooden legs, and then a round wooden body, and then wooden arms and hands, and then a wooden neck, and then a round wooden head," said the little man.

"And did he stick them all together and make *you*?" asked Big-Ears. "You've got funny eyes— and funny hair, too. What are they made of?"

"The old man made holes in my wooden head and then pushed blue beads into the holes," said the nodding man. "That's why I've got such bright blue eyes. He made my hair out of bits of fur from his cat's back. She said he could."

"Well—why are you running away?" asked Big-Ears, getting on his bicycle.

"Because it's so *lonely* with Old Man Carver," said the little man. "Besides—he's carving a lion now, and I don't like lions. I want to go and live somewhere where there are lots and lots of *people*."

10

"Then I really think you ought to live in Toyland," said Big-Ears. "You're not a brownie, so you can't live in my town. You're not exactly a toy either—but you're very like one. You'd better go to Toyland."

"I don't know the way," said the little nodding man, and his head nodded sadly.

"Well, I do," said Big-Ears. "Stand on the step of my bicycle—look, put your foot there—that's right—and I'll take you to catch the Toyland train."

11

The nodding man did as he was told. He nearly fell off when Big-Ears rode down the path, and he clutched at the brownie's pointed ears in fright.

"What's your name?" shouted Big-Ears, as they went along. "Hey, let go of my ears! Tell me your name."

"I haven't got one," said the nodding man. "What do you suppose my name ought to be, brownie?"

"Noddy, I should think!" said Big-Ears, nearly running over a fat beetle. "Look where you run, Beetle! Yes—I think your name is Noddy, little nodding man."

"I think so, too," said Noddy, happily. "Yes, I'm Noddy, of course. Ooooh—what's that?"

"That's the train whistling," said Big-Ears, pedalling at a tremendous pace. "We shall just catch it. I'll come with you if you like."

They rode into the station at top speed just as the train was rumbling in.

"All aboard for Toyland!" cried a voice. "All aboard for Toyland!"

THEY RODE INTO THE STATION AT TOP SPEED

13

2

## ALL ABOARD FOR TOYLAND!

THE train was a lovely one. It was a toy
train, of course, and it was made of
brightly-painted wood. The engine was red, with
a blue funnel and yellow wheels. The carriages
were all open; and dear me, how crowded they
were!

"Come on—get in!" said Big-Ears; and he
climbed into a very full carriage, pushed Noddy
in too, and dragged his red bicycle after him.

There were two dolls, a wooden soldier and a pink cat in their carriage.

"You trod on my tail," said the pink cat.

"Sorry," said Big-Ears. "Move up a bit, and take your tail out of the way. Sit down, Noddy."

Noddy nodded his round head, and stared with his blue bead eyes.

"What's he keep nodding for?" asked the wooden soldier. "Tell him to stop. Who is he, anyway?"

"He's Noddy," said Big-Ears. "He's going to Toyland. I'm not quite sure, but I think he's a toy. So he ought to go there."

"He's forgotten to dress himself this morning," said one of the dolls.

"I haven't forgotten," said Noddy. "I never do dress, because I haven't any clothes. I've only got my round wooden body."

"We'll get you some clothes in Toyland," said Big-Ears. "You don't look very beautiful with just your wooden body to go about in. Ah, we're off."

The engine gave a screech that made Noddy's head jerk up and down more than ever. Then the train rumbled off to Toyland, its bright wooden carriages jolting behind it, full of toys and pixies and brownies.

"Look! We're running through Monkey Town now," said Big-Ears. "See the monkeys everywhere?"

Sure enough, there were dozens and dozens of toy monkeys to be seen.

16

"LOOK! WE'RE RUNNING THROUGH MONKEY TOWN NOW,"
SAID BIG-EARS

17

When the train stopped at Monkey Station, three monkeys squashed themselves into the same carriage as Big-Ears and Noddy.

"You trod on my tail," said the pink cat, with a loud yowl. "Sorry. Keep it out of the way," said the monkey. "It's silly to leave it lying about. Move up, wooden soldier. Hello, who's this fellow with the nodding head?"

"I'm Noddy," said the nodding man. "I'm running away to Toyland!"

The train rumbled off again. "We come to Rocking-Horse Town next," said Big-Ears. "The rocking-horses never catch the train, though, because they can get along as fast as any engine by rocking to and fro, if they want to."

"Oooh—that must be Rocking-Horse Town over there," said Noddy. "My word—I'd like one of those nice to-and-fro horses."

"Well, that's a new name for them!" said one of the monkeys. "Now, let's see—where do we come to next?"

18

"Clockwork-Mouse Town," said the pink cat. "And I don't mind telling you that if a mouse gets in here I shall give it a very bad time!"

Only two mice got in, but neither of them was in the pink cat's carriage, so that was all right. She got out herself at the next station, which was Toy-Cat Town.

19

"Goodbye!" called the wooden soldier. "And remember not to leave your tail lying about!"

"Where do I get out?" whispered Noddy to Big-Ears. "This is all Toyland, isn't it? What station do I get out at? Is there a Nodding-Man Station?"

"No—you get out at Toy Town," said Big-Ears. "Ah—here we are. Toy Town! Come on, we get out here, my little wooden Noddy!"

20

## TOY TOWN

THE station at Toy Town was a big one, and it was full of people. Toy porters rushed up and down with barrows, dolls ran to catch the train, toy animals got into everyone's way, and worst of all a bouncing ball almost knocked Noddy over.

"That bouncing ball!" said Big-Ears, crossly. "It's not supposed to travel by train—it can quite well bounce for miles if it wants. Look out—here comes a top!"

A spinning-top bumped into Noddy, and sent him spinning, too. The top spun itself into a carriage and flopped down, lying still. The engine whistled and the train went off.

Noddy got up and dusted his wooden body down. "I do wish I had some clothes," he said. "Everyone is dressed so nicely that I feel dreadful. Why, even those teddy bears over there have blue ribbons round their necks."

"We'd better go and buy some clothes," said Big-Ears. "I mean—your wooden body is quite nice, but it does look sort of bare and cold. Hey, Teddy Bear—where are the shops?"

"Turn to the right and straight ahead," said the bear. "But if I were you I'd go to the market—it's much cheaper there."

So they went to the market. It was a lovely place, and very busy. Toy buses ran through it,

and toy cars and bicycles shot about everywhere. There were plenty of market-stalls too, selling almost everything.

"Now what kind of clothes do you want?" asked

22

Big-Ears, who was getting very fond of the funny little nodding man. "I'll lend you some money."

"How do you get money?" asked Noddy. "I don't really know what money is."

"It's something you get when you work hard," said Big-Ears. "Then you put it into your pockets and wait till you see something you want. Then you give it in exchange. You will have to work soon, then you can get money to buy heaps of things."

"I see," said Noddy. "Well, I'm strong. I can work *very* hard. I'll be able to pay you back quite soon, dear Big-Ears."

"Oh, I say—what lovely red shoes! Do you like those?" asked Big-Ears, stopping in front of

23

a shoe-stall. "Look—they've got blue laces. I believe they would fit your big wooden feet, Noddy."

Noddy put them on and laced them up. "*Just* my size!" he said. "Don't my feet look grand?"

Big-Ears paid for the shoes. The next thing they bought was a pair of bright blue trousers, rather wide at the bottom. Noddy was so pleased with them that he could hardly say a word. His head nodded madly.

"Goodness—you're beginning to look a very nice fellow," said Big-Ears, surprised. "Now for a shirt. We'll get you a red one, I think."

They found one, and then bought a yellow belt and a yellow tie to match. Noddy could hardly believe he was looking at himself when he suddenly caught sight of a mirror!

"I'm afraid I can't afford a coat," said Big-Ears, counting out his money. "But I've enough for a hat. Here's a hat-stall. Which would you like?"

"This is rather nice," said Noddy, picking up a blue doll's bonnet. Big-Ears laughed loudly.

24

"THIS IS RATHER NICE," SAID NODDY, PICKING UP A BLUE
DOLL'S BONNET

"*You* can't wear a bonnet! You're not a baby doll. Really, you don't know very much, Noddy."

"No, I don't," said Noddy, nodding his head sadly. "Well, you choose one for me, then."

"What about this?" said Big-Ears, and he picked up a pointed blue hat with a bell at the tip that jingled. Noddy was very pleased with it. He put it on top of his untidy hair, and looked

at Big-Ears out of bright blue eyes. Big-Ears nodded. "Yes—it suits you. Now you're all dressed up properly, Noddy."

"What do I do next?" asked Noddy anxiously, and then he jumped almost out of his skin.

A big toy policeman had come up to him.

"Are you a toy?" said the policeman, in a

booming voice. "Only toys are allowed to stay in Toy Town."

"I *think* I'm a toy," said Noddy, nodding his head in fright. "I know I don't belong to the fairy folk. Please let me stay here. I'm sure I'm a toy."

"You might be an ornament," said the policeman, sternly. "Like a china pig. That's an

27

ornament, unless it's a money-box pig, then it's a toy. You look rather like an ornament. Have you ever been stood on mantelpieces?''

"No, never," said poor Noddy.

"Have you ever been played with by children?" asked the policeman.

"No, never," said Noddy.

"Well, dear me—it seems as if you're not an ornament and not a toy either," said the policeman. "You'll have to come before the Court tonight, and we'll decide just *what* you are!"

4

## BIG-EARS HAS A GOOD IDEA!

NODDY was upset when the policeman walked away. He looked at Big-Ears. "What am I to do?" he said, his bell tinkling on his hat as he nodded his head in dismay.

"Oh, they'll say you're a toy all right," said Big-Ears. "Come on, now, we must find a house for you—just a little tiny one. Look, there are dolls' houses over there—we'll choose one."

They went over to them. There were big

29

houses and little houses, some with gardens and garages, and others without.

"There are curtains at all the windows," said Noddy, sadly. "I'm afraid they're all taken, and people are living in them."

Big-Ears knocked at some of the doors. But it was no good, there was a family in every one.

"Could you just let

Noddy live with you till he gets a house of his own?" asked Big-Ears. "Or do you know anywhere he could stay? He wouldn't mind sleeping anywhere—even in a garage—would you, Noddy?"

Noddy nodded, and his bell jingled merrily.

"Try at the toy farm," said a sailor doll who lived in a dear little house with his three children, Melia, Pip and Roundy. So they went to the farm, but the dogs barked so loudly at

30

THE DOGS BARKED SO LOUDLY THAT THEY WERE AFRAID
TO OPEN THE GATE

31

them that they were afraid to open the gate.

"It's no good. I shan't be able to find anywhere to live here," said Noddy, sadly. "I'll have to take the train again and go back to Old Man Carver."

"No. I shan't let you," said Big-Ears. "Oooh—*I* know what we'll do!"

"What?" said Noddy.

"We'll go and get a box of bricks and *build* a house!" said Big-Ears. "Haven't you noticed the dear little houses here and there, built of toy bricks? You can get boxes of bricks that have little doors and windows with them and a roof and chimneys to fit on."

"My goodness—let's go and get one, then!" said Noddy, excited. So they went to the back of Toy Town, where there was a great shed, like an aeroplane shed.

But there weren't any aeroplanes inside— instead there were boxes of bricks for building houses and castles and even shops!

A toy soldier stood on guard outside. "What do you want?" he asked,

saluting very smartly indeed. Noddy saluted back, and his bell rang loudly.

"We want a box of bricks to build a very small house," said Big-Ears. "Just big enough for Noddy. A back room for a bedroom and a front room to live in. No stairs. We can't manage those."

"I've just the thing for you," said the soldier. "It's called House-for-One. Here it is. Quite cheap, too."

"You'll have to send me the bill," said Big-Ears. "I haven't any more money. Come on,

Noddy, we'll put the box on our shoulders, and
go and find a nice place for the house!"

So they carried the box, panting and puffing
because it was very heavy. They came to a dear
little street with houses of all kinds up and down it.

"Look," said Big-Ears. "There is a space
between those two houses—just big enough to
build yours!"

They undid the box and looked at the bricks
inside. "Better read the directions," said Big-Ears,
unfolding a paper in the box. "I've never built
a house before. My, this is going to be FUN!"

34

5

## NODDY BUILDS HIS HOUSE

IT *was* fun building the house of toy bricks.
Noddy wasn't very clever when they began.

"Let's put the roof on first," he said. "Then
if it rains we shan't get wet whilst we build the
walls, shall we?"

"Don't be silly, Noddy," said Big-Ears. "We
must build the walls *first*. Look, here are some
flat bricks to make the floor. We'll lay those
first."

So they laid those. Then they began to build the walls. It was really quite easy. Noddy was so pleased with himself that he built a whole wall in no time.

"You've forgotten to leave a space for the door," said Big-Ears. "How are you going to get in? And, oh dear, I'm just as bad—I've forgotten the window on my side!"

At last the walls were up, all the bricks fitting nicely on top of one another. Spaces were left for the door and the windows.

AT LAST THE WALLS WERE UP, ALL THE BRICKS FITTING
NICELY

"*Now* for the roof," said Big-Ears. "Got hold of it? Heave-ho, and up she goes!"

And up went the nice red roof, and sat neatly on top of the four walls.

"How are we going to put on the chimneys?" said Noddy. "We'll have to borrow a ladder now."

"I'll ask next door," said Big-Ears, and he went and rapped on the little yellow front-door of the house on the left.

It was opened by a rather fat teddy bear. "I'm Mr Tubby," said the bear. "What do you want?"

"Could you lend us a ladder, please?" asked Big-Ears. "We're just finishing building our house."

"Certainly. I'll give you a hand," said Mr Tubby, and brought out a little ladder. He put it against a wall, ran up it, and looked down. "Hand me the two chimney-pots," he said. "I'm good at putting on chimneys.

38

He put them on very well, and then he helped
them to put in the two windows and the door.

"Well, really it looks very nice," said Mr Tubby, stepping back on poor Noddy's toe. "Oh, sorry! Did I hurt you?"

Noddy's head nodded hard, and the bear ·really thought he had hurt him very much. He didn't know that Noddy always nodded.

"Come and have a cup of tea with me," he said. "Nothing like a cup of tea if anyone treads on your toe!"

6

## TEA WITH MR TUBBY

MR Tubby's house was rather grand. It had stairs, so there was an upstairs and a downstairs, and it had a nice little bathroom. Noddy didn't even know what that was!

"He doesn't even know what a bath is!" said Big-Ears. "Well, Noddy, you have to fill this bath with water and then get into it. See? Then you wash yourself all over."

"But it would spoil my nice new clothes,"

said Noddy; and Tubby and Big-Ears laughed
loudly at him.

"You take your clothes
off first, silly!" said
Big-Ears.

Mr Tubby had a nice bear-wife. She was just
as fat as he was, and wore lovely clothes. She
had a full red skirt and a pretty green shawl.
Tubby just wore yellow trousers and a ribbon
round his neck.

They had a very good tea. Noddy was hungry
and so was Big-Ears. Through the side-window
they could see the little house they had built.
Noddy began to feel very, very happy.

He had run away. He would live here in Toy
Town in the dear little house he had built him-

42

THEY HAD A VERY GOOD TEA. NODDY WAS HUNGRY AND
SO WAS BIG-EARS

self. He would make friends with Mr and Mrs Tubby. He would go to work. He would ask Big-Ears to stay with him just as soon as ever he had some furniture and a bed. Oh, what a lot of things he would do!

"I'm going to be very happy here," he said suddenly, helping himself to his third jammy bun, and he nodded his head more quickly than ever.

"Don't forget that you've got to go before the Court of Toys tonight, and they'll decide whether you are a toy or not," said Big-Ears. "If they say you're not, you won't be able to stay."

"Oh dear—and will my nice little house belong to somebody else?" said Noddy, tears coming suddenly into his eyes.

"I'm afraid so," said Mr Tubby. His fat little wife patted Noddy on the shoulder.

"If they say you're not a toy you can come and spend the night with us, and go away tomorrow morning," she said kindly. "I shan't want to stay anywhere in Toy Town if I'm to go away," said Noddy. "Oh, I do hope they'll be kind to me."

44

7

## NODDY AND THE NOAH'S ARK

A FTER tea Noddy thought he would like to take a walk through Toy Town. So he and Big-Ears set off together.

Toy Town was really a marvellous place. The houses were so pretty, and the dolls that lived in them looked so busy, hanging clothes out on the line, chattering to their neighbours, and bringing home their shopping.

45

"I've never seen so many people," said Noddy, nodding his head happily. "To think I might live here and know them all!"

"Look—there's the castle where the soldiers live," said Big-Ears; and Noddy saw an enormous wooden castle, with towers and a drawbridge. Lead soldiers and wooden ones too, were in the castle yard, drilling. Big-Ears and Noddy went to watch them.

"I'm going to see what that funny thing is over there," said Noddy at last.

"Oh, it's only the Noah's Ark," said Big-Ears. "Don't go. I still want to watch the soldiers."

"Well, you stay there, then, and I'll come back to you," said Noddy, and he went off to the Noah's Ark. He had never seen one and he didn't know what it was at all. There it stood, like a great wooden boat with a roof and walls! Who lived in it?

Noddy walked right up to it. He saw that there was a door into the Ark. "I really must climb up and peep inside the door!" he thought. "I want to know who lives there."

So he climbed up and opened the door—and dear me, out came dozens of wooden animals, all marching in pairs, most excited to be let out so unexpectedly!

Mr Noah and his wife had gone out shopping, and had shut all the animals safely inside the Ark. And now there they were, pouring out, almost knocking poor Noddy over as they came!

"Go back!" he cried. "Go back!" But they wouldn't, and goodness knows what would have happened if Mr and Mrs Noah hadn't come back just then and met all their animals streaming out of the Ark.

"Good gracious!" cried Mrs Noah, and she clapped her hands sharply. "Go back at

48

OUT CAME DOZENS OF WOODEN ANIMALS, ALL MARCHING
IN PAIRS

once! What are you thinking of? Sheep, do you want to be smacked? Cats, shall I set the two dogs at you? Br-r-r-r-r! Go back at once!"

They all turned and scurried back as fast as they could go—all except one!

The lion didn't go back. He ran behind a bush and crouched there, waving his tail from side to side. The lioness went back into the ark wondering where the lion had gone. But nobody else missed him at all.

Noddy was frightened by what he had done. He was just about to go up to Mr Noah and tell him it was his fault that all the animals had been let out, when the door of the Ark was slammed in his face.

"Oh dear," said Noddy. "How was I to know they kept so many animals in there?"

50

He thought he had better go back to Big-Ears at the castle. He was just making his way there when he heard a scream.

A little doll stood nearby, pointing at the Noah's Ark lion. She screamed again. The lion was angry, because he thought that everyone would come running and he would be made to go back into the Ark. He badly wanted to go off on his own for a while.

He leapt out at the little doll, roaring, hoping she would run away and stop screaming. He wouldn't have hurt her for the world, because he liked little dolls—but he did want to stop her screaming.

Noddy didn't know the Noah's Ark lion was just a kindly old fellow, who only wanted a little walk by himself. He really thought the lion was going to hurt the tiny doll.

Noddy was very frightened. He shook and shivered and trembled. But he knew he must try to save the little doll. So what do you think he did?

He rushed at the surprised lion, shouting and yelling. He threw his hat at him. He pulled off his new shoes and threw those at him, too. One hit the lion on the nose, smack!

The lion was terrified. He gave a yelp and rushed to the Ark, knocking on the door with one of his wooden paws, anxious to get safely inside.

Noddy put his arm round the little doll. "It's all right. I scared him away. He won't come back again."

The little doll's mother came running up. "I saw you scare away that bad wooden lion! Thank you, thank you! How brave you are! What's your name?"

"Oh—that's nothing. Er—it was my fault that the lion escaped," said Noddy, his head nodding hard. "Er—I must just get my hat and shoes."

He got them and fled away to Big-Ears. Dear, dear, what an adventure to have all on his own!

## 8

## IS NODDY A TOY, OR NOT?

NODDY and Big-Ears went back to their little house. Big-Ears got his bicycle ready to ride all the way home. But, just as he was going, there came a knock at the door.

"Ratta-tat, TAT!"

It was the policeman. "Time to come before the Court," he said to Noddy. "I'm afraid it won't have been much good building this house. I don't believe you are a toy!"

Noddy went sadly to the Court with Big-Ears pedalling beside him. Oh dear!

They came to a neat little police-station built of toy bricks. Inside was a big court-room, packed with policemen and toys. Six soldiers were there, too.

"The soldiers will take you out of Toyland, if you are sent away," whispered Big-Ears, and Noddy looked very miserable.

Everyone got up suddenly as a very solemn-looking person came in and took a grand chair up on the platform. She was the judge, with a big wig hanging to her shoulders. Noddy was so frightened that his head began to nod very quickly indeed.

"Stand out here," commanded the judge, and Noddy stood out, trembling. Everyone looked at him.

"Now, we have to decide whether you are a toy or not," said the judge. "What have you got to say for yourself?"

"I *feel* like a toy," said Noddy.

"And look how he nods his head," called out Big-Ears. "Just like a toy! Some toys growl if you press their middles. Some turn head over heels when you wind them up. Some can bounce and some can spin. Noddy can nod!"

"Then he's a TOY!" shouted everyone.

"Silence!" said the judge, rapping on her table.

"Now, suppose we say he *is* a toy . . . but is he a GOOD toy? We don't want bad ones here."

She turned to Noddy. "Are you a good toy? Have you done anything wrong since you have been here?"

56

"I LET THE NOAH'S ARK ANIMALS OUT. BUT I DIDN'T KNOW
THEY LIVED THERE"

Noddy was just about to say *no*, but as his head was nodding hard, the judge thought he meant *yes*, he *had* done wrong.

"*What* have you done wrong?" she asked, very sternly.

Noddy remembered that he had let the Noah's Ark animals loose. Was that wrong? Yes, it must have been.

"Please, miss," he said, "I let the Noah's Ark animals out. But I didn't know they lived there."

"Very wrong," said the judge. "I'm afraid I . . ."

But before she could finish what she was going to say, an excited little doll popped up and waved her hand eagerly.

"Please, Miss Judge, I want to say something. That's the little nodding man who rescued my child from the Noah's Ark lion. He's brave! He's good! He was frightened, but he went to save my little girl!"

58

Then everyone clapped and stamped and cheered loudly. The judge rapped her table again. She was smiling.

"Ah—that's a nice thing to hear!" she said. "Noddy *is* a toy. He's a *good* toy. He's a *brave* toy! Noddy, you can live in Toyland, and have the house you built!"

Well, wasn't that lovely? Big-Ears laughed and shouted, and thumped Noddy on the back. Everyone crowded round him.

59

"Welcome to Toyland! Welcome Noddy!"

And that was how Noddy came to Toyland, and went to live in the dear little house he had built. How glad he was that night to shut his own front-door and curl up in a chair that Mr Tubby had lent him.

"I'm in my own little house! I'm so happy! I'll work hard and buy lots of things for my house. I'll pay Big-Ears back all the money he lent me!" Noddy nodded and nodded as he thought about it all.

"I'll have heaps of adventures," he said to himself. "Oh, heaps and heaps!"

And so he will. I'm going to tell you all about them another day.

# THE NODDY LIBRARY

*Noddy Books* are available through all good Booksellers or from the BBC Shop (Newcastle). For telephone enquiries please call 091 222 0381. Mail order address: PO BOX 1QX, Newcastle-upon-Tyne NE99 1QX.